making something from everything

ASHLEY BRYAN'S DISCARD
puppets

Ashley Bryan

photographs by
Ken Hannon

photographs edited by
Rich Entel

Atheneum Books for Young Readers
New York London Toronto Sydney New Delhi

To dear friends Dr. Rich Entel and Rhoda Boughton,
and to the memory of my sister, Elaine Martindale
—A. B.

Special thanks to: Soos Valdina;
Dunedin Fine Arts Center DFAC,
Dunedin, Florida (where Ashley had
the show that inspired this book);
Catherine Bergmann, Curator DFAC;
Irwin Entel; Kris Hannon; Henry Isaacs;
and Jane Burke.
—R. E.

atheneum

ATHENEUM BOOKS FOR YOUNG READERS

An imprint of Simon & Schuster Children's Publishing Division

1230 Avenue of the Americas, New York, New York 10020

Copyright © 2014 by Ashley Bryan

Photographs of raw materials (above and pp. 6–7) by Michael McCartney and Ellice Lee

All other photographs by Ken Hannon

All rights reserved, including the right of reproduction in whole or in part in any form.

ATHENEUM BOOKS FOR YOUNG READERS is a registered trademark of Simon & Schuster, Inc.

Atheneum logo is a trademark of Simon & Schuster, Inc.

For information about special discounts for bulk purchases, please contact Simon & Schuster Special Sales at 1-866-506-1949 or

business@simonandschuster.com.

The Simon & Schuster Speakers Bureau can bring authors to your live event. For more information or to book an event, contact the Simon & Schuster

Speakers Bureau at 1-866-248-3049 or visit our website at www.simonspeakers.com.

Book design by Ann Bobco

The text for this book is set in Hank BT.

The hand puppets for this book have been made from raw materials.

Manufactured in China

0414 SCP

First Edition

10 9 8 7 6 5 4 3 2 1

CIP data for this book is available from the Library of Congress.

ISBN 978-1-4424-8728-4

ISBN 978-1-4424-8729-1 (eBook)

AUTHOR'S NOTE

I grew up in New York City during the Depression years. My sister and I would pick up cast-off things on the sidewalks. We had endless ideas of how we could re-create these objects and give them new life.

As an adult, walking the shores of the Cranberry Isles, I did what I did in New York City, what most people walking the shore do: pick up shells, bones, driftwood, nets, and sea glass. From those collections, my family of hand puppets was created. They greet you now in this book.

My puppets are happy that you are spending time with them. They sing out to you, "Bright thanks!"

Ashley Bryan

Ashley,
what will you
name me when
my garment is
complete?

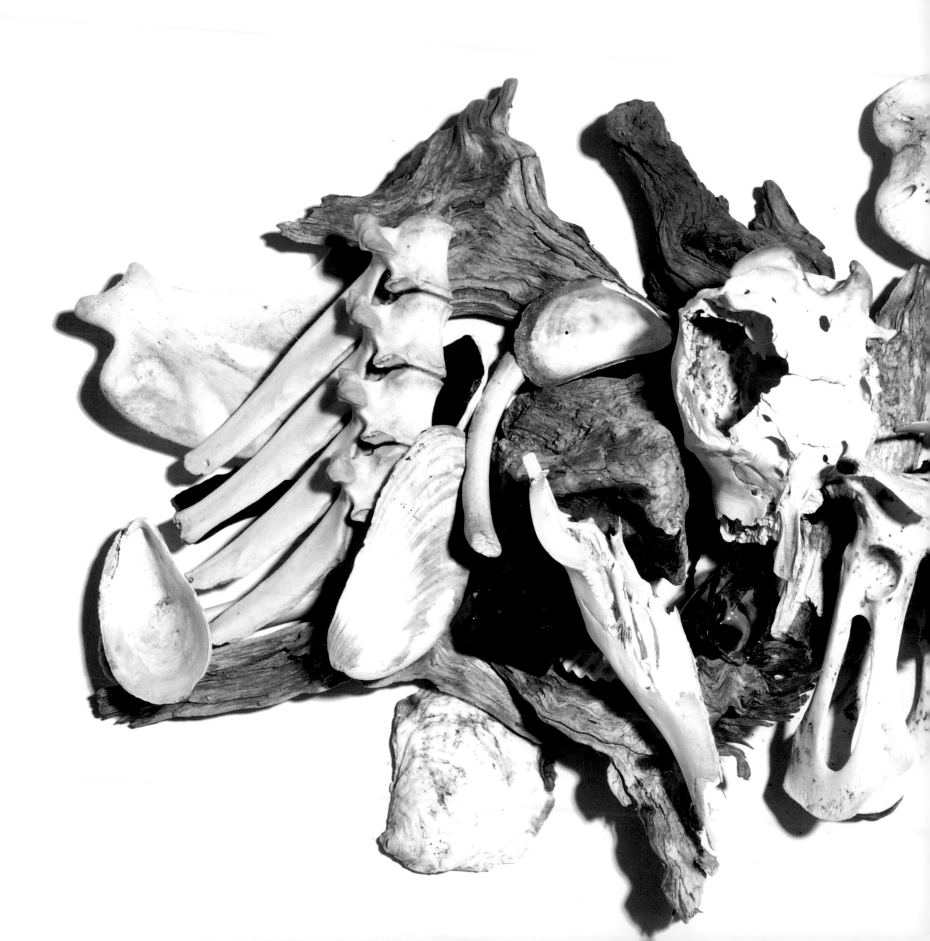

These treasures,
Washed in from the sea,
Are cast-off challenges to me.
I cannot rest till I create
A life that we may celebrate.

Spider   Pepukayi   Animata   Ayodele

Kwesi   Chipo   Seitu   Nkosi

Ayodele
Joy Comes Home

It doesn't take
Much scrutiny
To know that I
Come from the sea.

My lobster beak,
Shell head, bone jaw
Combine in ways
Not seen before.

We're startled by
The mystery
Of how new life
Can come to be.

The answer's in
The revelation:
Creation's joy is
Imagination.

Kwesi
Conquering Strength

Stew bones fashioned for a trunk,
Rib bones for a tusk;
Shoulder bones, my perfect ears,
Opal eyes a must,
Old corduroys that washed ashore,
With shells, seaweed, a plant.
I'll journey now to Africa
A proper elephant.

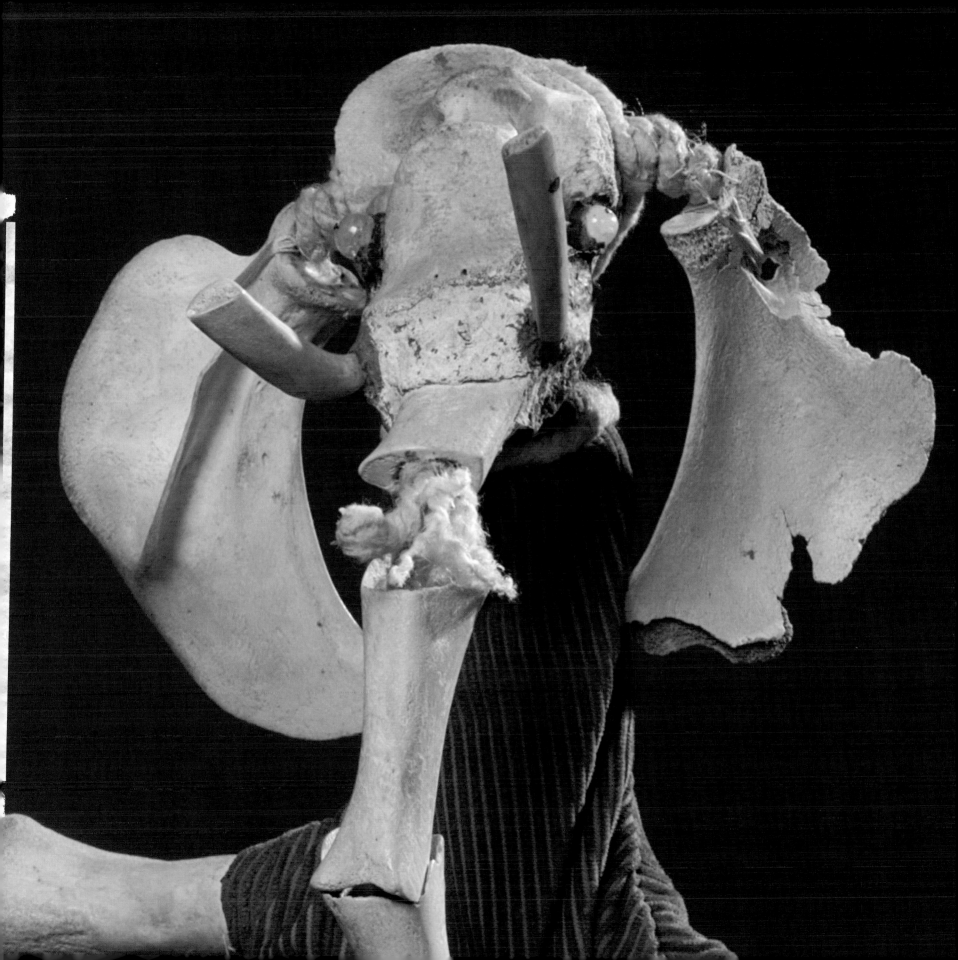

Pepukayi
Wake Up

Head bone, bone face,
Laughing metal jaws,
Long string nose, so neatly traced,
I'm a frog. I croak outdoors.

I scan the shore
With seashell eyes,
For waves have offered
Me a prize.

I'm wedded to a mermaid;
She sews my orange dresses.
Her love is stitched
To every square—
My webbed hands
Comb her tresses.

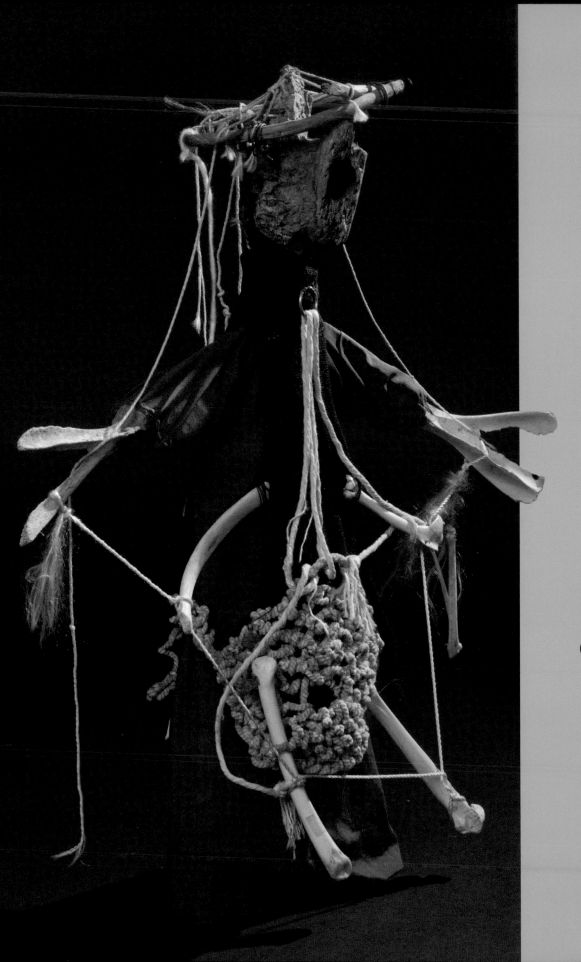

Spider
Trickster

I'm Spider Anansi.
I spin without rest
A close web of stories
For cradle and nest.
Spinning fine stories
Of tricks that I play,
Mischievous adventures
Come home now to stay.

Animata

Good Character

Regal and tall,
Shells, pearls, and all—
A glass for a crown,
Designed upside down—
My long purple dress
In the style I wear best—
I come from the sea.
I am roy-al-ty.

Chipo

Gift

My coconut head
Is filled with ideas
Of silver ships sailing
With plums, apples, pears.

Good fruits are the cargo
For cakes, tarts, and pies,
The idea I've chosen
Is peach pits for eyes.

Seitu
Artist

Let every nation
Praise and sing
Of glories that
Their artists bring.

I dress in silks, embroideries.
Others, homespun jute.
Still we are all fine artists
No matter what the suit.

A thousand years from now
They'll say,
"Those long-gone artists
Live today."

Nkosi
Ruler

I walk out of dreams,
Through tall trees of the wood.
I wander and wonder:
Is all waking good?
Are my dreams the real
Or is this world my dream?

I saddled this question,
A jockey for eyes.
I don't have the answer,
Though rulers be wise . . .
You answer the question—
I'll give you three tries.

Natambu   Osaze   Babatu   Mombera

Cazembe   Jojo   Lubangi   Olutosin

Cazembe

Wise One

I'm a night owl.
My acorn husk eyes
Stare through thick glasses.

With outspread wings
I'm feathered for flight,
An echo of insects,
Surer than sight,
Ping to my beak.

When poised and full
I relive the music and wisdom
Of winged lines,
A feast of poems
I've memorized.

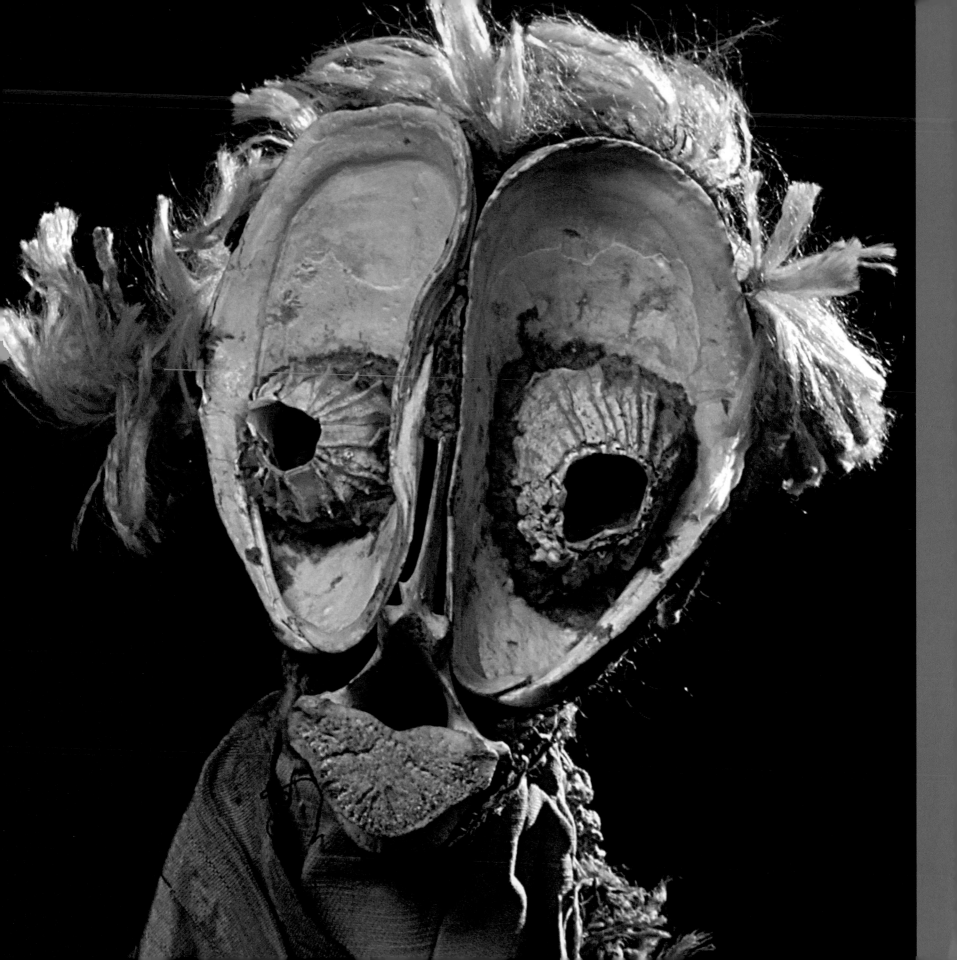

Osaze
Whom God Loves

When we first met
I thought you were old.
Your manner, so gentle,
So quiet, so sage,
I was certain it had to come
Only with age.

Your shapely shell hands
Embraced me in greeting.
You said, "To be loved,
To make peace, to be caring
Are not about age."

Your knowing eyes
Saw through to my heart;
No longer strange.
We became friends.
The same age.

Babatu
Peacemaker

I'm director of these actors
In this picture book new play.
I'll call these actors to the stage
And let them have their say.

We're a repertory company.
We are trained for any role.
We are proud of our ensemble;
"Be the best"—our stated goal.

I'm peacemaker;
Trained, wise counselor.
Should any conflicts start,
I listen to their stories
Till we're one in mind and heart.

Mombera

Man of Adventure

I sport a hip regalia
Of leather, hemp, and suede.
Said I sport a hip regalia,
Shiny leather, hemp, and suede.
You dig that I am watchful.
Yeah, my eyes are watchband made.

I drive a sleek convertible,
I clock each covered mile.
I drive a sleek convertible,
I time each covered mile.
My hair is tousled by wild winds;
Kids copy it for style.

Can't help inspiring new ideas,
As timely as my clocks.
Can't help inspiring new ideas,
Yeah! Timely as my clocks.
I let no hours close me in,
I strike out from the box.

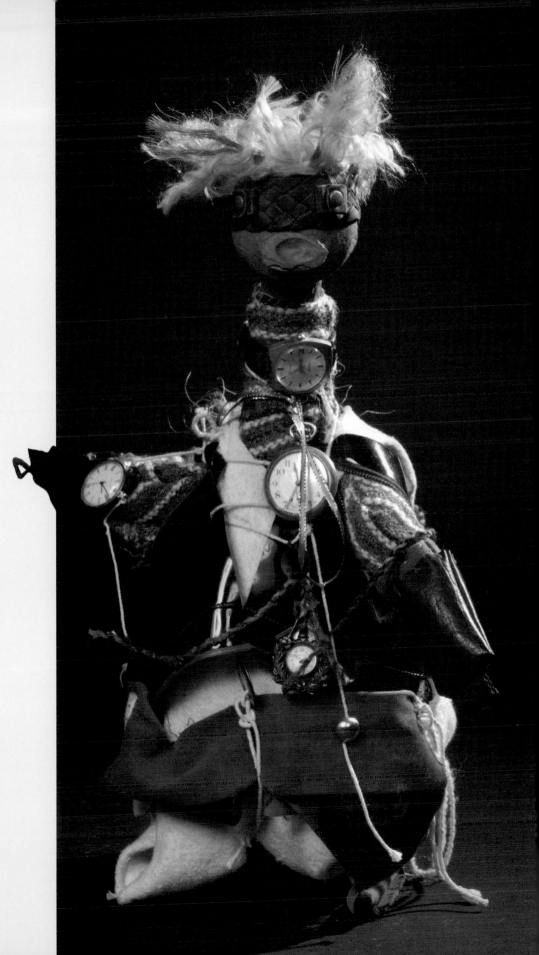

Natambu
Man of Destiny

My strong distinguished bedpost head
Sprouts unruly hempen hair.
But I've trained my wishbone whiskers,
Which I daily comb with care.

I apprenticed as a printer,
Soon was master of my trade,
Decorated ten times ten
With ribbons,
Apt rewards for types I've made.

I am blessed to love my calling,
Proud of honors that I get.
May I live to cast and set at last
The perfect alphabet.

Jojo

Storyteller

In every finger of my glove
I tap tall tales of peace and love.
The fingers of my well-gloved hands
Store stories told in foreign lands.

In every patch of my quilt gown
Are myths and fables,
Long passed down.
I honor sources and make clear
The origin of tales I share.

I always wished to sell good things,
I thought of all the joy that brings.
What better product for a seller
Than marketing as a storyteller.

Lubangi
Born in Water

I am a sea-glass mermaid,
Sparkling as bright seas.
The shards from broken bottles
Fill my head with melodies.

I compose starfish musicals
Sung by mermaids in salt water.
The leading singer in the cast
Is my operatic daughter.

Three current acts
Were vocalized
Before landlubbers on shore,
To salty sprays of applause
And to shouts of more!
"Encore! Encore!"

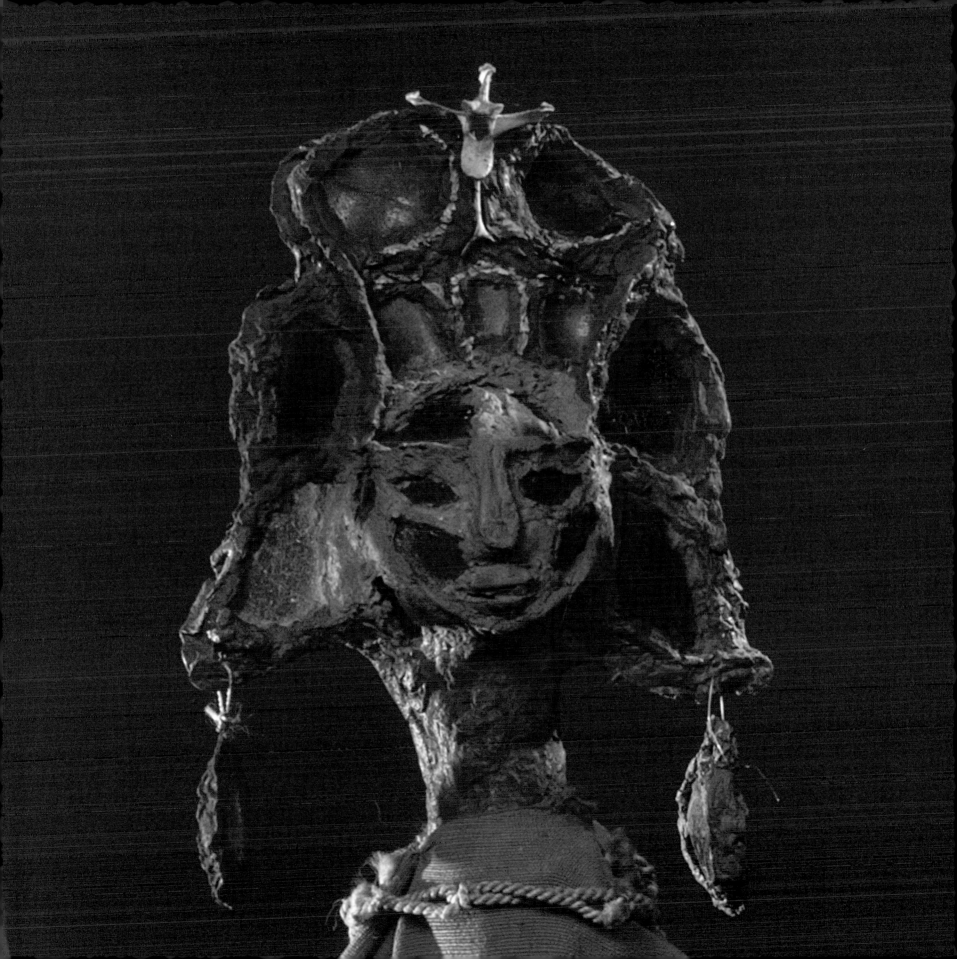

Olutosin

God Be Praised

Who were the first singers?
Would you like to guess?
All had voices
But birds sang best.

Trees and flowers
Sing in the wind.
Why did all this
Singing begin?

In the beginning,
Song was raised
For joy in life
The Lord
Be praised.

All singers rejoice,
All songs are blessed,
There's no competition
But birds sing best.

Ewunike   Moriba   Dedan   Afiba

Kitaka   Changa   Barnabe   Mayimuna

Ewunike

Fragrant

My hairstyle is admired
By folks around the world,
But stories told
About my brush
Would make your
Straight hair curl.

I disinfect such stories,
Wear sterilized new clothes,
Choose only
Fine French fragrances
To tantalize your nose.

I'm always antiseptic.
I stand out in a crowd.
I'm a pure and proper puppet,
And all sing my praise aloud.

Afiba

By the Sea

There's a good chance
If you live by the sea,
You'll become a bonehead fisherman
Just like me.

My two sons are fishermen,
My daughter loves the trade.
The fishers buy her fishnet hats,
Her college costs were paid.

She's taught us all the science
Of oceanography,
So that our daily harvest
Does not deplete the sea.

Kitaka
Good Farmer

If you set out to prove your mettle,
You need not be made of steel,
Although my brass bedhead,
Electric socket–neck,
Make me stand out in the field.

I farm organic fruits and greens,
My fork hands scratch the earth.
My tin topknot nozzle sprinkles well,
And brings my crops to birth.

My thumbtack eyes
Then scan the skies
For days to praise the land.
Brother Changa comes
Pounding drums
In his Caribbean steel band.

Dedan
Town Dweller

When building a house,
Constructing it sound,
Start from the top
And build down to the ground.

Learn from mistakes.
Some steps built on air
May end in the bathtub.
You don't want them there!

My head's a wood bedpost.
My hat frames a crown
That revels in nonsense;
Turns thoughts upside down,

I scribble in space,
Then scramble each station.
A roof is easier to replace
Than a poor foundation.

Changa

Strong as Iron

Whenever I, Changa, appear,
Steely eyes, steps of iron,
A clashing of metal,
The smashing of cymbals,
A clanging of bells,
The clapping of spoon hands.
This litany of sound
Raises a din in the air.
Allow no distraction—
As I come near
Shout out loud and clear:
Changa's here!
Changa's here!

Mayimuna

Expressive

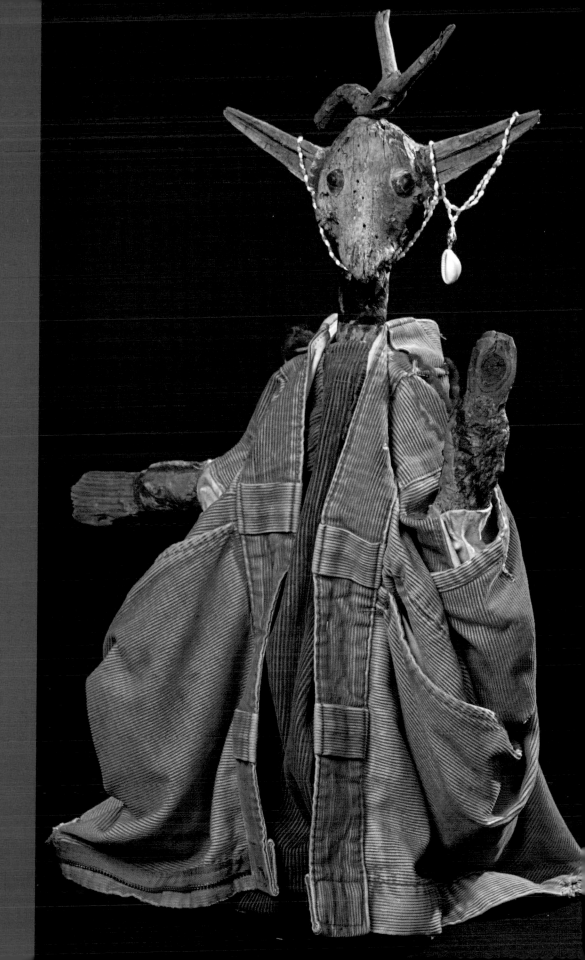

I auditioned for a part
In an upcoming play.
The casting director
Noted my shapely face,
My pointed ears,
My hair, like sticks,
Splitting the air,
My bashful demeanor.

Everything about me
Led to a part,
A character unlike me.

I am amazed
That the acting art
Could change me.
Teach me how to convince you
That I am
Who I am not.

Abayomi   Chinyelu   Marka   Ashaki

Zawdie   Jaramogi   Andito   Chioneso

Chinyelu
Invincible

Come, my friend, travel with me
To ancient and modern lands.
Through jungles, over mountains,
Across windswept desert sands.

There's magic and mystery
In these marble eyes,
These whitened bones,
My hide an impenetrable silk sleek cloak.
I'm Ox of the Wonderful Horns.

Of warriors who meet me,
There's none who can beat me.
I trounce the valiant foe who tries;
In my horns the secret lies.

Touch the horns, close your eyes,
Make a wish—Surprise! Surprise!
Your wish will come true.
If you wish as you should,
For all things that are good.

Ah! I knew that you would.

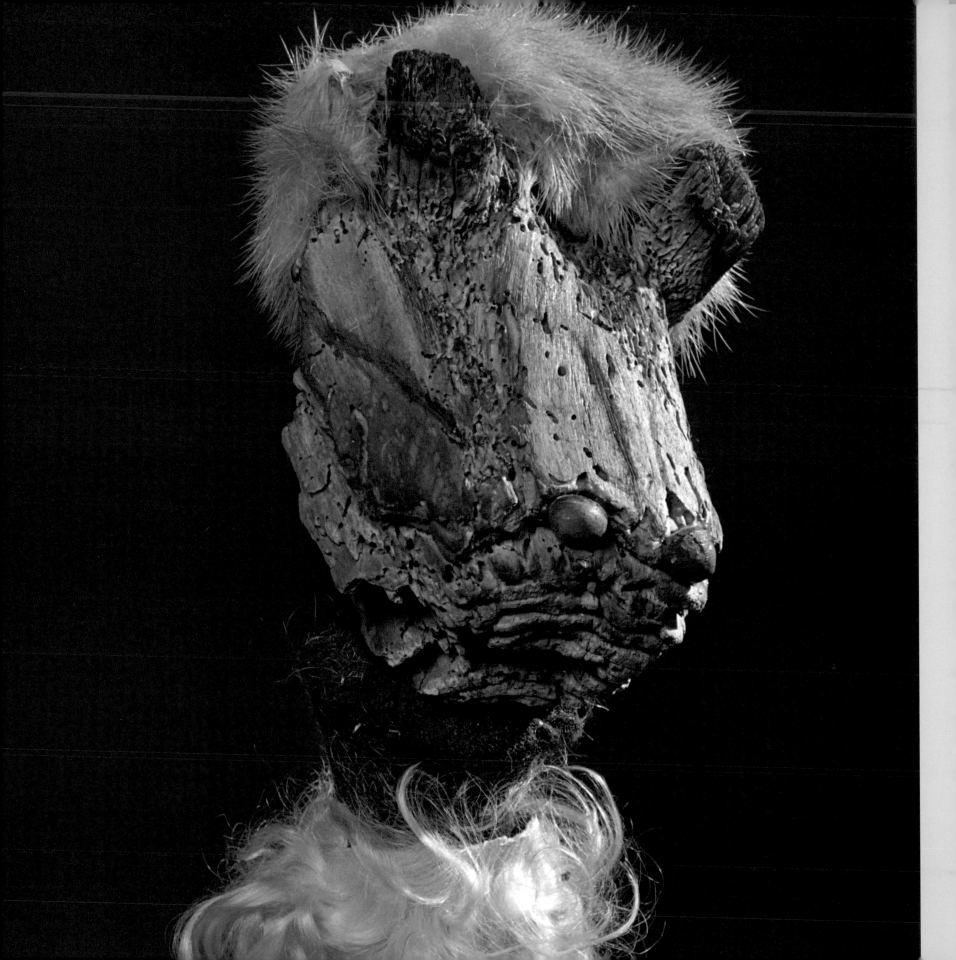

Marka

Steady Rain

I am a cow.
I munch green grass.
Grass needs the rain
Moo, moo! Please last.

I turn green grass
Into white milk.
Don't ask me how;
I'm just a cow.

Ashaki
Beautiful

When I lay down to sleep,
Papier-mâché stories
Awake in my head.
My dreams take off
To golden lands.
There I live in rooms that gleam,
I hear birds singing
As I weave cloths of yellow threads.

When I awake
My whole world glows.
I find the golden dreams,
Like halos,
Have gone to my head.

Abayomi

Ruler of People

My driftwood oak head
Washed up from the sea;
Has branches like antlers
That stick up for me.

I thought I would drown,
But they steered me to shore.
To fine furs they next led me;
Now I'm dressed and secure.

I stick up for others
So all may live free;
I'm grateful for antlers
That stick up for me.

Serwaa

Jewel

I live a life
Of honesty
Because you always
See through me.

My whiskey head
Wine-beer sea glass
Transparent gems
That give me class.

So, please, no scolding.
Do not rant
Because my head's intoxicant.

I'm colorful, sober
As can be,
Because you always
See through me.

Zawdie

Chosen Leader

Serwaa and I,
Born of sea glass,
Were childhood sweethearts.
I knew it would last.

One day the puppets gathered,
They took up a vote
To name as their leader
A classy man of note.

Votes were counted.
And then with one voice
They named *me*
Their man of choice!

As chosen leader
I chose for life
My sea-glass
Sweetheart—
Serwaa—for my wife.

Jaramogi

Traveler

In order to compose myself
I walked shores far and wide;
My nets and shells,
My corded neck
Were gathered at high tide.

My head was shaped
With pointed wood,
My right and left arms too.
I then set sail for storied seas
In search of yarns for you.

I spin my sea tales
Sound and clear,
Regaled from many angles.
No social nets will be my snare
Or catch me in triangles.

Andito

Great One

Them bones, them bones,
Them dry bones.
Hear the Word
Sung in glory,
The everlasting story.
Hear the Word
Oh! Hear the Word.

Them bones, them bones,
Them dry bones.
Oh! Wear them.
Oh! Bear them.
They chant the Word
Flown down from above
On wings, on wings—
Wings of a dove,
Wings of a dove.

Them bones, them bones,
Them dry bones.
Oh! Hear the Word,
Hear the Word.
When you hear it,
Share it, share it.
Rejoice the Word
Heard from above,
Is LOVE is LOVE
Is LOVE LOVE LOVE.

Njonjo
Holy Man

Stroking my fishnet beard,
I bless the daily gifts
That others take for granted:
Sunrise, sunset,
Birds gliding on currents of air,
Air that I breathe in, breathe out.

I'm clothed from head to foot
In robes of health and joy.
I look up to the sky
With outstretched arms,
I embrace life,
I say my daily prayer.
Thank you,
Thank you.

Spirit Guardian

My family of puppets
Freely seek me and call.
I'm their Spirit Guardian.
I watch over them all.

We are born of cast-off pieces
And, like magic, brought alive
By your own imagination.
That's the gift
By which we thrive.

Our reality is the treasure,
The adventures that we share
When you close this book
And look up,
You'll see puppets everywhere.

AFTERWORD

Public service is an honorable calling. Those who serve our country in times of war are accorded our highest honors and are frequently awarded our highest accolade: hero. But we know heroes don't always carry any sort of authority—not a badge nor a gun nor a dazzling uniform that requires instant respect. Most of us lead daily lives of grace and dignity, seeking to trust our neighbors, support our communities, and share the burden of those in the troubles of natural or man-made disasters.

Where is the reward for the citizen who puts her refuse in the recycling bin? Probably at the same ceremony where the old woman smiles at the baby or the teenager gives his seat to the gentleman in the bow tie. Probably not many places, yet we work not for reward or award but for the goodness of the thing.

Artists are heroes. They share a vision of a greater us. They lay their emotions like so many plums in the sun to be dried by the light of truth and caring.

I am a puppet. My name is Wambui: I sing because I acknowledge the possibility of flotsam on the shore reaching the loving hands of a master artist.

—Nikki Giovanni

For his dear friend
Nikki Giovanni,
Ashley created
Wambui. His gift
inspired her to
write the following
poem:

Wambui
Singer of Songs
(for Ashley Bryan)

I am a puppet.
My name is Wambui:
I sing because I acknowledge
the possibility
of flotsam on the shore
reaching the loving hands
of a master artist.

In the double-spread lineups, there are three puppets without poems: Moriba, Barnabe, and Chioneso. They are waiting for you to create poems for them. There are also three puppets that snuck into the book that do not appear in any lineups. . . . Can you find these puppets?

As the puppets shaped themselves, it seemed to Ashley that they each selected their own names from various countries of Africa.
Below is a history of when each puppet was "born" and from which country.

Ayodele, on pages 10–11: Made in 1973, Yoruba
Kwesi, on pages 12–13: Made in 1971, West Africa
Pepukayi, on pages 14–15: Made in 1975, Ma-Shona people
Spider, on pages 16–17: Made in 1972, East Africa
Animata, on pages 18–19: Made in 1974, West Africa
Chipo, on pages 20–21: Made in 1976, Ma-Shona people
Seitu, on pages 22–23: Made in 1962, East Africa
Nkosi, on pages 24–25: Made in 1982, South Africa
Cazembe, on pages 28–29: Made in 1966, Central Africa
Osaze, on pages 30–31: Made in 1956, Benin
Babatu, on pages 32–33: Made in 1960, West Africa
Mombera, on pages 34–35: Made in 2004, East Africa

Natambu, on pages 36–37: Made in 1984, Yoruba
Jojo, on pages 38–39: Made in 1956, East Africa
Lubangi, on pages 40–41: Made in 1957, East Africa
Olutosin, on pages 42–43: Made in 2008, Yoruba
Moriba, on page 44: Made in 2011, West Africa
Barnabe, on page 45: Made in 1955, West Africa
Ewunike, on pages 46–47: Made in 2005, East Africa
Afiba, on pages 48–49: Made in 1956, West Africa
Kitaka, on pages 50–51: Made in 1981, Central Africa
Dedan, on pages 52–53: Made in 1968, East Africa
Changa, on pages 54–55: Made in 1982, Central Africa
Mayimuna, on pages 56–57: Made in 2007, West Africa

Chioneso, on page 59: Made in 2009, Ma-Shona people
Chinyelu, on pages 60–61: Made in 1980, West Africa
Marka, on pages 62–63: Made in 2006, West Africa
Ashaki, on pages 64–65: Made in 1955, West Africa
Abayomi, on pages 66–67: Made in 1964, West Africa
Serwaa, on page 68: Made in 1967, West Africa
Zawdie, on page 69: Made in 1963, East Africa
Jaramogi, on pages 70–71: Made in 2011, East Africa
Andito on pages 72–73: Made in 1957, West Africa
Njonjo, on pages 74–75: Made in 1983, East Africa
Spirit Guardian, on pages 76–77: Made in 2003
Wambui, on page 79: Made in 2008, East Africa

The Book of African Names—as told by Chief Osuntaki, Drum and Spear Press—
has even more names that you might give the puppets you will make!